You'll Soon Grow into Them, Titch

Pat Hutchins
You'll Soon Grow

into Them, Titch

RED FOX

OTHER PICTURE BOOKS
BY PAT HUTCHINS

Changes, Changes
Clocks and More Clocks
Don't Forget the Bacon!
The Doorbell Rang
Good-Night, Owl!
Happy Birthday, Sam
King Henry's Palace
One-Eyed Jake
One Hunter
Rosie's Walk
The Silver Christmas Tree
The Surprise Party
Titch
Tom and Sam
The Very Worst Monster
Where's the Baby?
The Wind Blew
Tidy Titch
Silly Billy
My Best Friend

A Red Fox Book. Published by Random House Children's Books,
20 Vauxhall Bridge Road, London SW1V 2SA.
First published in Great Britain in 1983 by
The Bodley Head Children's Books
First published in paperback by Puffin 1985
Red Fox edition 1994.
3 5 7 9 10 8 6 4 2
First published by Greenwillow Books New York 1983
© Pat Hutchins 1983
Printed in China
RANDOM HOUSE UK Limited Reg. No. 954009
ISBN 0 09 920711 7

FOR AMY

Titch needed new trousers.

His brother Pete said,
"You can have my old trousers,
they're too small for me."

"They're still a bit big for me,"
said Titch.

"You'll soon grow into them,"
said Pete.

And when Titch needed a new sweater,

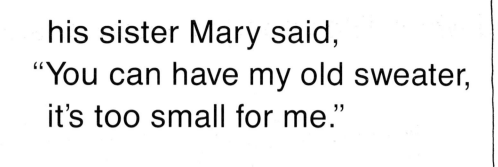

his sister Mary said,
"You can have my old sweater,
it's too small for me."

"It's still a bit big for me,"
said Titch.

"You'll soon grow into it,"
said Mary.

And when Titch needed new socks,

they both said,
"You can have our old socks,
they're too small for us."

"And I'll soon grow into them,"
said Titch.

"I think," said Mother, "that Titch should have some new clothes."

So Dad and Titch went shopping.

They bought a brand-new pair of trousers,

a brand-new sweater,

and a brand-new pair of socks.

And when Mother brought their brand-new baby home, Titch wore the new clothes.

"There," said Titch,
"he can have my old trousers,

and my old sweater,

and my old socks.
They're much too small for me!"

"They're a bit big for him,"
said Pete and Mary.

"He'll soon grow into them,"
said Titch.